BIBLE STORIES *for* TEENS

The Relatable Devotional to Connect God's Word with the Real-Life Challenges of Anxiety, Identity, and Purpose

EMELINE KRISCE

Published by
GRAPEVINE BOOKS

www.grapevinebooks.com
email: contact@grapevinebooks.com

Ordering Information:
Quantity sales: Special discounts are available on quantity purchases by corporations, associations, and others. For details, reach out to the publisher.

First published by Grapevine Books, 2025

Contents

OLD TESTAMENT

NEW TESTAMENT

1 Created with Purpose

In the beginning, there was only silence. No waves crashing. No birds calling. No colors or shapes or shadows. Just complete stillness. Then, in a moment that split the darkness open, God spoke three simple words that changed everything.

"Let there be light."

Light rushed in like a flood. Darkness scattered. The world began to glow with warmth and color. With each word God spoke after that, more life appeared. Oceans rolled into place. Stars lit up the sky like a million tiny lanterns. Trees stretched upward. Animals filled the land and sea.

But creation was not complete.

Using His own hands, God formed Adam from the dust and breathed life into him. Adam opened his eyes to a world fresh and bright. God gave him a role, a home, and a purpose.

Then God created Eve, crafted with the same care and intention. She was made equal, valued, and deeply loved. When she took her first breath, she stepped into a world with the presence of God Himself.

In Eden, nothing was rushed. Nothing was broken. Adam and Eve were fully known and completely accepted. They lived with identity, meaning, and connection. No pressure to perform. No insecurity. God looked at them and saw that His creation was good. He saw purpose in them.

And the same God who shaped the sun and sculpted mountains shaped you. Not by mistake. Not by accident. With care. With intention. With a purpose your life is slowly uncovering.

P
R *God, help me remember that I was created intentionally.*
A *Show me your purpose for me and teach me to walk in it every day.*
Y

Reflection

Where do you struggle most to believe that your life was created with intention and value from the very beginning?

2 The First Broken Choice

It began with a question. A quiet one. Soft enough that Eve almost missed it, but sharp enough to slip into her thoughts.

"Did God really say...?"

The serpent spoke with a tone that felt calm, almost friendly. Eve paused. She knew the truth. God had given them every tree except one. Life in the garden had been simple. Peaceful. Perfect. Nothing had ever made them question God's goodness.

But temptation rarely arrives as something scary. It comes disguised as something interesting. Something almost reasonable.

The serpent leaned in. "You will not really die. God knows that if you eat it, your eyes will be opened."

Eve looked at the fruit. It seemed harmless. Bright. Beautiful. She held it and felt curiosity stirring. Adam watched, torn between what he knew and what he suddenly wondered. One bite. One moment of choosing the whisper over God's voice.

Eve tasted it. Adam followed her. And everything shifted. The peace of the garden cracked. Shame rushed in like a storm. They hid from God, the One who had always walked with them in the cool of the day.

Still, God came searching for them, not with anger, but with sadness. He called out to them, offering a chance to step into the light, even though everything had changed.
Their story reminds us that doubt still whispers today. It still twists what God says. But God still comes looking for us. His love reaches for us even when we run.

P
R *God, help me recognize temptation when it tries to sound harmless.*
A *Give me strength to choose what is right and stay close to You.*
Y

Reflection

How can you stay anchored in God's truth when you feel tempted or unsure?

3 Noah Stands Strong

The world had grown loud with cruelty. Violence filled the streets. People mocked goodness and chased whatever they wanted. But Noah lived differently. He chose God when everyone else refused.

One day, God spoke words that changed Noah's entire future.

"Make yourself an ark."

It made no sense. There was no storm. No rising water. No warning signs in the sky. But Noah didn't argue. He didn't stall. He started building. Piece by piece. Day after day.

People laughed at him. They pointed at the giant boat in his yard and called him ridiculous. Noah kept going anyway. Faith sometimes feels lonely, and Noah knew that better than anyone.

When the rain finally came, it came hard. The ground shook. Water rushed across the earth. The people who had mocked him felt fear rise for the first time. But Noah and his family were safe inside the ark, held steady by the God they trusted.

For months, the world stayed underwater. But Noah kept believing that God was not finished. When the dove returned with a fresh olive leaf, hope rose again.

Noah stepped out of the ark onto a quiet, renewed world. God set a rainbow in the sky as a promise that destruction would never win the final word.

Noah's story reminds us that faith sometimes asks us to trust before we understand. To stand firm when others drift. To build when others mock.

P
R *God, help me stand strong even when I feel alone.*
A *Teach me to trust You more than the voices around me.*
Y

Reflection

What is one thing God may be asking you to build or start even if others do not understand?

4 Abraham Steps Out

Abraham did not grow up hearing God's voice. He did not live in a place where people worshiped the Lord. Yet one day, everything changed. Out of nowhere, God spoke and gave him a command that would shake his entire world.

"Go to the land I will show you."

No map. No details. No timeline. Just a call to step into the unknown. Abraham looked around at his home, his family, and everything familiar. Leaving would mean uncertainty. It would mean questions. It would mean risk.

But Abraham chose trust.

He packed his things. He gathered his family. He walked forward without knowing what waited ahead. Every step was an act of faith. Every mile was proof that trust grows when we move, not when we stay still.

God promised Abraham a future far bigger than he could imagine. Descendants as countless as stars. A nation formed through him. Blessings that would reach the whole world. Abraham had no proof yet, but he believed.

The journey was long. Some days were confusing. Other days felt impossible. At times, Abraham stumbled. At times, he questioned. But he kept walking, one faithful step at a time.

And God kept His promise.

Abraham's story teaches us that faith is not about having all the answers. It is about trusting the One who does.

P
R *God, give me courage to step into the unknown when You call me.*
A *Help me trust Your leading even when the path feels unclear.*
Y

Reflection

What fears hold you back from trusting God the way Abraham did?

5 Hagar Is Seen

Hagar never expected her story to matter. She was a servant, often ignored, often mistreated, pushed into decisions she never chose. When Sarah grew jealous and angry, Hagar fled into the wilderness with nothing but fear driving her forward.

There, alone in the desert heat, she broke down. No plan. No protection. No place to go. She felt invisible, unwanted, forgotten. But that is when God met her in a way she never saw coming.

The angel of the Lord spoke to her with gentle strength.

"Return to your mistress."

It was not the future she expected, but God also gave her something she desperately needed. A promise. A future for her son. A reminder that she was not forgotten.

Then Hagar said words no one else in Scripture had spoken before.

"You are the God who sees me."

In that lonely desert, she learned that God does not overlook the hurting. He steps into the wilderness moments and calls us by name.

Hagar returned with strength she did not have before. She carried hope with her. And even though her circumstances were still complicated, she was no longer alone. God had met her in the emptiest place and filled her with purpose.

Her story still speaks today. When you feel unnoticed or misunderstood. When life feels unfair. When loneliness feels loud. God sees you. He knows your pain. He walks toward you, not away.

P
R *God, thank You for seeing me when I feel invisible.*
A *Remind me that my story matters to You, even on the hard days.*
Y

Reflection

When have you felt unseen or forgotten, like Hagar in the wilderness?

6 Jacob's New Identity

Jacob had spent years running. Running from his mistakes. Running from the brother he tricked. Running from who he used to be. But the night before he faced Esau, everything inside him felt unsettled. Fear pressed hard. Regret felt heavier than his bags.

That night, someone appeared in the darkness. Not a thief. Not an enemy. Someone far stronger. Jacob wrestled with him through the night, refusing to let go. Sweat, dirt, and desperation mixed together as he fought for something he couldn't fully explain.

Then the stranger said a simple line.

"Let me go."

Jacob held tighter. **"I will not let you go unless you bless me."**

The man looked at him and changed everything with one powerful sentence. "Your name shall be Israel." Jacob had been labeled a deceiver his entire life, but God gave him a new identity. A new beginning. A name that meant God fights.

When morning came, Jacob limped away from the encounter, but he was different. He walked toward Esau with new courage. He walked with honesty instead of pretending. He walked knowing God had changed who he was at the core.

Jacob's story shows us that God meets us in the wrestling. He shapes us in the struggle. And He teaches us that our past does not get the final say.

P
R *God, meet me in the areas I struggle and shape me into who You*
A *created me to be.*
Y

Reflection

What identity or label from your past do you need God to rewrite?

7 Joseph Stays Faithful

Joseph's life had gone from favorite son to forgotten prisoner faster than he ever imagined. One moment he wore a colorful coat. The next he was thrown into a pit, sold by his own brothers, and taken far from home. But even in Egypt, God was with him.

While Joseph worked faithfully, lies pulled him down again. He was falsely accused and thrown into prison. It felt unfair. It felt cruel. It felt like God had gone silent. But Scripture says, "The Lord was with Joseph." Even in the darkest place.

Joseph refused to let bitterness win. He served others. He used his gifts. He interpreted dreams. He stayed faithful when everything around him felt broken.

Years later, God lifted him from the prison to the palace. In one day, Joseph went from prisoner to second-in-command over all Egypt. And when famine hit, the same brothers who betrayed him came seeking help.

Joseph could have chosen revenge, but he didn't. He said something powerful instead: **"You meant evil against me, but God meant it for good."** He saw purpose in the pain. He saw God's hand in the places he never wanted to be.

Joseph's story teaches us that setbacks do not cancel God's plan. Delays do not erase His promises. And faithfulness in the hard places shapes us for the future God is preparing.

P
R *God, help me stay faithful even when life feels unfair.*
A *Remind me that You are with me in every season.*
Y

Reflection

What area of your life feels like a setback, and how might God be working through it?

8 Moses Meets God

Moses had settled into an ordinary life. Shepherding sheep. Walking desert paths. Keeping to himself. He didn't think his story mattered anymore. He didn't expect anything new. But one day, on a quiet mountainside, something caught his eye.

A bush was burning, but it did not burn up.

As Moses stepped closer, a voice called out to him from the flames.

"Moses, Moses."

It startled him. It humbled him. It was the voice of God. Moses removed his sandals, standing on holy ground, his heart pounding. God told him He had seen His people suffering. He heard their cries. And Moses was the one He chose to lead them out.

Moses doubted himself. He stuttered. He questioned. He felt unqualified. But God answered him with a short, powerful promise:

"I will be with you."

Moses had nothing impressive to offer, yet God still chose him. God wasn't looking for perfection. He was looking for willingness.

Moses walked away from that mountain with a calling bigger than his fears. His life changed because he listened to God in an unexpected moment.

His story reminds us that God often meets us in ordinary places, speaks into our insecurities, and calls us forward even when we feel unready.

P
R *God, speak to me in the quiet places and help me trust that You*
A *can use me even when I feel unqualified.*
Y

Reflection

When have you sensed God speaking in an unexpected or ordinary moment?

9 The Red Sea Path

The Israelites had finally escaped Egypt, but freedom lasted only a moment before panic hit. Behind them, Pharaoh's army thundered forward. In front of them, the Red Sea blocked their path. Fear spread quickly. People shouted. Some wanted to turn back. Others blamed Moses.

The situation looked impossible.

Then Moses spoke words meant to steady their hearts.

"Stand firm and see."

The people quieted. Moses raised his staff toward the sea. The wind roared. Water split apart, lifting into towering walls. A dry path appeared where waves once crashed. God had made a way no one could have imagined.

The Israelites walked forward, step after trembling step, surrounded by miracle. When they reached the other side, the waters closed and the Egyptian army was gone. The people who had once been terrified now broke into song, praising the God who fought for them.

Sometimes God waits until the last moment to show His power. Not to scare us, but to remind us that His strength is far greater than our fear. The Red Sea teaches us that God can open paths where none exist and lead us through situations that look impossible.

Your Red Sea moments are not the end. They are places where God does His most powerful work.

P
R *God, help me trust You when I face impossible situations.*
A *Show me the path You are opening even when I cannot see it yet.*
Y

Reflection

What situation in your life feels like a Red Sea moment with no clear way forward?

10 Choosing God's Ways

The Israelites stood at the base of Mount Sinai, watching lightning flash and hearing thunder rumble across the sky. God was speaking with power, giving Moses the Ten Commandments. These were not rules meant to trap them. They were meant to guide them toward a life filled with peace, trust, and freedom.

In the middle of everything God said, one line stood out as steady and simple.

"You shall have no other gods."

It was clear. Direct. Protective. But while Moses stayed on the mountain, the people grew restless. They gathered around Aaron and demanded a new god they could see and touch. Aaron melted their gold and shaped a calf. Music filled the camp. Dancing followed. They chose noise over truth. Excitement over obedience.

When Moses returned, his heart broke. The people had traded God's voice for something shiny and empty. They forgot who rescued them. They forgot the freedom they had been given.

Choosing God's ways is not always dramatic. Sometimes it simply means staying patient when others rush. Sometimes it means holding onto truth when easier options appear. God's commands are not heavy. They are meant to lead us toward life, not away from it.

Israel's story reminds us that distractions can look harmless, but they pull our hearts away from the One who loves us most.

P
R *God, help me choose Your ways even when distractions seem*
A *easier or more exciting. Keep my heart focused on what is true.*
Y

Reflection

What distracts you most from staying close to God's voice?

11 Jericho's Walls Fall

Jericho looked completely impossible. Thick walls, guarded gates, armed soldiers watching from above. Israel had come so far, but now they stood in front of a barrier no human strength could break. Joshua waited for God to give a plan, expecting something intense or strategic. Instead, God told him something very simple.

"March around the city."

No fighting. No shouting. No rushing. Just walking. One lap each day for six days. On the seventh day, seven laps. It seemed slow and strange, but Joshua obeyed. The people followed quietly, step after step, trusting that God was doing something even if they could not see it.

On the final lap, Joshua lifted his voice and gave the command God had given him.

"Shout, for the Lord has given you the city."

The people shouted. The ground trembled beneath their feet. Cracks split through the stone. Dust rose into the sky. Jericho's mighty walls collapsed like they were nothing at all. What was impossible to them was simple for God.

Jericho teaches us that obedience sometimes looks small and repetitive. It looks like patience when we want speed. It looks like trust when we want control. God often works in ways that do not match our expectations, but He never fails to do what He promises.

P
R *God, help me trust Your plans even when they do not look like the*
A *solutions I expect. Strengthen my faith as I obey You.*
Y

Reflection

How do you respond when God asks you to be patient instead of taking action right away

12 Deborah Leads Boldly

Israel was trapped under cruel oppression. The enemy commander, Sisera, controlled the land with iron chariots and overwhelming power. People lived in fear. Roads were empty. Hope felt distant. But in the middle of all that darkness, God raised up an unexpected leader: Deborah.

She was a prophet. A judge. A woman who listened closely to God. The people trusted her wisdom, and she settled disputes under a palm tree in the hill country. One day, God gave her a message for Barak, Israel's commander.

"Go, for God will deliver."

Barak hesitated. He felt unsure and afraid. He looked at Deborah and said he would only go if she came with him. Deborah agreed, stepping into danger with confidence rooted in God, not herself.

When the battle began, God threw Sisera's army into confusion. Chariots crashed. Soldiers scattered. The enemy fled. Israel won a victory they never believed possible.

Deborah's story reminds us that leadership is not about muscles or titles. It is about courage. It is about listening to God when others freeze in fear. It is about stepping forward even when the path is risky.

God uses people who trust Him, regardless of age, gender, or background. Anyone willing to listen can lead boldly.

P
R *God, help me develop courage that comes from You. Teach me*
A *to lead with wisdom, humility, and confidence in Your presence.*
Y

Reflection

What qualities do you think make someone a good and godly leader?

13 Gideon's Hidden Courage

Gideon never saw himself as brave. When Israel was suffering under Midianite attacks, Gideon hid while threshing wheat, hoping the enemy would not find him. Fear pressed in from every side. Then a messenger from God appeared and greeted him with surprising words.

"The Lord is with you."

Gideon looked around, confused. He felt weak, overlooked, and unsure. He questioned God. He doubted himself. But God saw courage buried inside him, courage Gideon did not recognize yet. God told him he would lead Israel to victory.

To prove His power, God reduced Gideon's army from thousands to only three hundred men. It sounded impossible. Yet Gideon obeyed. Armed with torches and trumpets instead of swords, they surrounded the Midianite camp at night. When Gideon gave the signal, the men broke their jars, lifted their torches, and shouted.

"The sword of the Lord."

The enemy panicked and fled. God brought victory through a man who once hid in fear.

Gideon's story shows us that God sees strength in us even when we feel small. He does not measure courage by confidence. He measures it by willingness. When we trust Him, He turns ordinary people into bold ones.

P
R *God, help me see myself the way You see me. Give me courage to*
A *step out even when I feel afraid.*
Y

Reflection

How does Gideon's story change the way you think about courage?

14 Samson's Strength

Samson's strength was legendary. It was a gift from God, announced before he was even born. The angel who spoke to his parents gave a simple promise.

"He shall begin to save."

Samson grew up powerful, bold, and fearless. But strength without wisdom can become dangerous. Samson often acted impulsively. He chose excitement over caution. His decisions pulled him into unhealthy relationships, especially with Delilah, who secretly worked with the Philistines. Samson trusted her even when she repeatedly tested him.

Eventually he revealed the secret of his strength. Delilah betrayed him. Samson was captured, blinded, and taken prisoner. Everything that once made him confident was gone. Yet in the darkness of the prison, Samson discovered something he had missed before. Strength was not really about muscles. It was about dependence on God.

Samson prayed sincerely for the first time, asking God to give him strength again. During a celebration, Samson stood between two pillars and leaned into them with renewed faith. God answered his prayer. With all his might, Samson pushed, and the building collapsed, bringing Israel victory.

Samson's story shows that God can redeem even our worst mistakes. Strength is not meant to make us proud. It is meant to point us back to Him.

P
R *God, teach me to use my abilities with wisdom.*
A *Help me rely on You instead of my own strength or impulses.*
Y

Reflection

What distracts you most from staying close to God's voice?

15 Ruth's Loyal Love

Ruth's world changed overnight. Her husband died, leaving her in grief, uncertainty, and deep loss. Naomi, her mother-in-law, urged her to return to her own homeland so she could rebuild her life. It was the logical choice. But Ruth looked at Naomi with a loyalty far stronger than fear.

She spoke one of the deepest commitments recorded in Scripture.

"Where you go, I will go."

Ruth walked beside Naomi all the way to Bethlehem, choosing love over comfort and faithfulness over convenience. She was a foreigner with no safety, no money, and no guarantee of acceptance. To survive, Ruth gathered leftover grain in the fields, hoping someone would show kindness.

Boaz noticed her first by her character, not by appearance. He protected her, provided food for her, and honored her loyalty. Over time, God brought Ruth and Boaz together, weaving a story of hope from a beginning of heartbreak.

Ruth eventually became part of the family line of King David and later Jesus Himself. A woman with no status and no certainty became a vital part of God's plan for the world.

Ruth reminds us that faithfulness in small moments can open doors to a future bigger than anything we imagine.

P
R *God, help me love with loyalty and kindness, even when it costs me*
A *comfort. Make my heart steady and faithful like Ruth's.*
Y

Reflection

When have you chosen loyalty or love even when it was difficult?

16 Samuel Hears God

The tabernacle was quiet at night. Lamps flickered softly. The air felt still. Young Samuel lay down to sleep, tired from serving Eli all day. Nothing about the night seemed unusual until a voice echoed through the darkness.

"Samuel."

Samuel sat up quickly. He thought Eli had called him, so he ran to the priest's room. But Eli shook his head. "I did not call." Samuel returned to bed, confused but calm.

Then it happened again. "Samuel."

He rushed to Eli once more. Same response. No call. No instruction. Only confusion. On the third time, Eli realized something Samuel did not yet understand. God was speaking. The Lord had chosen to call a boy in the quiet when the rest of Israel had stopped listening.

When Samuel heard his name a fourth time, he whispered the words Eli taught him.

"Speak, for Your servant hears."

In that moment God began shaping Samuel into a prophet. A boy who once served quietly now heard messages that would guide kings, confront nations, and reveal God's heart. Samuel learned that God's voice often comes softly. Not in storms. Not in fire. Often in the quiet moments when we least expect Him.

God does not wait for perfect people. He speaks to willing hearts, no matter their age or experience. Samuel's story teaches us to stay open, stay listening, and stay ready.

P
R *God, open my ears to hear You. Help me recognize Your voice above*
A *all the noise around me.*
Y

Reflection

If God spoke to you tonight, what area of your life do you think He would bring up first?

17 David Faces the Giant

The battlefield was filled with fear. Israel's soldiers stood frozen as the giant Goliath shouted insults across the valley. He was huge, armored, and confident. He challenged Israel daily, daring anyone to step forward. No one moved.

Then David arrived. A shepherd boy carrying bread for his brothers. He heard the giant's insults and felt something rise inside him. It was not fear. It was conviction. David remembered the God who had helped him protect his sheep. The God who gave him courage when lions attacked.

David walked to King Saul and said confidently, "Your servant will fight him." Saul offered David armor, but it weighed him down. David chose what he knew God had used before: a sling, five stones, and faith.

As he approached Goliath, the giant laughed loudly. David replied with a simple, powerful truth.

"The battle is the Lord's."

David swung his sling. The stone flew fast, striking Goliath in the forehead. The giant fell face down, and the entire valley shifted from fear to victory. One boy changed the battlefield because he trusted God more than the size of the enemy.

David's story reminds us that courage is not about how big we are. It is about how big we believe God is. Giants fall when faith stands firm.

P
R *God, give me courage to face the giants in my life and confidence*
A *to trust Your strength more than my fear.*
Y

Reflection

What practical step could you take this week to face something that scares you?

18 David Finds Forgiveness

David had been a hero, a king, and a man after God's heart. But even strong leaders make tragic mistakes. In a moment of weakness, David made choices that harmed others and dishonored God. He tried to hide what he had done, but the guilt grew heavier each day.

Then God sent Nathan the prophet. Nathan told a story that exposed the truth, and David suddenly saw the weight of his sin. He did not argue. He did not make excuses. He whispered a confession that still echoes today.

"I have sinned against the Lord."

David felt broken, ashamed, and humbled. But instead of running from God, he ran toward Him. He wrote prayers filled with sorrow and honesty, like the words in Psalm 51. He asked God to create a clean heart inside him and restore the joy he once had.

God forgave him. The consequences were real, but grace was greater. David learned that forgiveness does not erase the past, but it rebuilds the future. God used him again, not because he was perfect, but because he was repentant.

David's story teaches us that sin does not have the final word. Failure does not define us. God offers forgiveness that reaches into the deepest parts of our lives.

P
R *God, help me bring my mistakes to You honestly. Clean my heart*
A *and restore the joy that comes from walking closely with You.*
Y

Reflection

What is one area of your life where you need honesty rather than hiding?

19 Solomon Asks for Wisdom

Solomon was young when he became king. The kingdom felt large, the responsibilities heavy, and the expectations overwhelming. One night God appeared to him in a dream and offered an incredible invitation.

"Ask what I shall give you."

Solomon could have requested anything. Riches, long life, victory in battles. But he thought about the people he was called to lead. He felt the weight of guiding a nation and whispered a request that revealed the heart God had placed inside him.

"Give Your servant an understanding heart."

God loved Solomon's request. He gave him wisdom greater than anyone before or after. Solomon became known for decisions filled with clarity, fairness, and insight. People traveled from far nations just to hear his judgments. His wisdom became legendary.

But Solomon's story is more than his brilliance. It reminds us that wisdom begins with humility. It begins with recognizing we cannot navigate life alone. God honors those who seek insight instead of power, guidance instead of control.

Wisdom does not make life perfect, but it helps us make choices that lead to peace, integrity, and purpose. Solomon shows us that the best things we can ask God for are the things that help us live well.

P
R *God, give me a wise and understanding heart. Help me make*
A *choices that honor You and bless the people around me.*
Y

Reflection

If God asked you the same question He asked Solomon, what would you request first?

20 Elijah's Low Moment

Elijah had just witnessed one of the greatest miracles in Israel's history. Fire fell from heaven when he prayed. The people turned back to God. The prophets of Baal were defeated. Yet shortly after this victory, fear overwhelmed him. Queen Jezebel threatened his life, and Elijah ran into the wilderness, exhausted and discouraged.

He collapsed under a tree and prayed words full of sadness.

"It is enough now."

Elijah felt alone, drained, and convinced his work did not matter. But God did not scold him. God cared for him gently. An angel woke him, offering food and water. Elijah slept and ate again. Rest came before answers.

Then God led him to a mountain. Elijah waited for God to speak. A powerful wind tore through the rocks. Then an earthquake shook the ground. Then a fire blazed. But God was not in any of those dramatic displays.

After the fire came a gentle whisper.

That was where God spoke. Elijah realized God meets us in quiet moments, not only in miracles. God reminded Elijah that he was not alone and that his work still mattered. Strength returned, not through power, but through presence.

Elijah's story teaches us that emotional lows are not signs of failure. Even faithful people experience exhaustion. God meets us where we are, speaks softly, and restores us one step at a time.

P
R *God, meet me in my low moments. Help me rest,*
A *listen, and remember that I am never alone with You.*
Y

Reflection

What emotions have been weighing you down recently that you need to bring to God?

21 Elisha Sees God's Help

Elisha woke up early, just like any other morning. But his servant stepped outside and froze. Enemy soldiers surrounded the entire city. Horses, chariots, armed men everywhere. It looked hopeless. The servant rushed back inside, panic filling his voice.

"Alas, my master, what shall we do?"

Elisha remained calm. He prayed quietly and then spoke a line filled with quiet courage.

"Fear not, for God is here."

The servant was confused. All he saw were enemies closing in. Elisha placed a hand on his shoulder and prayed again. "Lord, open his eyes." Suddenly the servant gasped. God opened his spiritual eyes, and he saw a sight more powerful than any army. Surrounding the hills were horses and chariots of fire. Heaven's army stood ready.

When the enemy advanced, God struck them with blindness. Elisha walked out calmly, led them away, and then prayed for their sight to return. Instead of destroying them, Elisha showed mercy. The enemy soldiers were fed and sent home unharmed. After that, they never attacked again.

Elisha's story reminds us that what we see is not all there is. God works in ways that are hidden to us. Sometimes fear closes our vision. Sometimes stress blinds us. But God surrounds His people with protection we may never notice.

Faith does not always remove the problem, but it lets us see that God is already present in the middle of it.

P
R
A
Y

God, open my eyes to see Your help, especially when I feel surrounded or overwhelmed by challenges.

Reflection

How would your reactions change if you believed God was already surrounding you with help?

22 Hezekiah's Brave Prayer

The king of Assyria threatened Jerusalem with terrifying confidence. His army was huge. His reputation was fierce. Messengers shouted threats at the people, trying to fill them with fear. They mocked God. They mocked Hezekiah. They promised destruction and captivity. The city felt hopeless.

Hezekiah did not answer with anger or fear. Instead, he carried the enemy's letter to the temple, spread it out before God, and prayed a powerful, honest prayer.

"Lord, You alone are God."

This simple declaration changed everything. Hezekiah admitted the danger. He acknowledged the strength of the enemy. But he placed the entire situation before God with humility and trust. That night, God moved in a way no soldier could have predicted. Scripture says an angel went out and struck down the Assyrian forces. When morning arrived, the threat was gone. Not because Jerusalem was strong, but because Hezekiah prayed boldly.

Hezekiah's story teaches us that brave prayer is not loud or dramatic. It is honest. It places fear into God's hands instead of handling it alone. The enemy's threats had been loud, but Hezekiah's quiet trust was stronger.

God still meets us when we bring our fears to Him directly. He still answers prayers spoken in humility and courage. Hezekiah reminds us that the battle is not always fought with strength. Sometimes it is fought on our knees.

P R A Y

God, teach me to bring my fears to You first. Give me confidence to trust You even when threats feel overwhelming.

Reflection

What fear or pressure would you lay before God if you physically placed it in front of Him like Hezekiah did?

23 Josiah's Young Revival

Josiah became king at only eight years old. The nation had forgotten God. Idols filled the land. People followed their own ways instead of God's commands. Josiah could have ignored it. He could have followed the traditions of the kings before him. Instead, he made a quiet, bold decision to seek God.

As Josiah grew older, he ordered repairs on the temple. During the work, the priests discovered a lost scroll. It was the Book of the Law, the very words God had spoken to Israel. When Josiah heard it read aloud, his heart broke. He realized how far the nation had drifted. He tore his clothes as a sign of grief and humility.

One line from Scripture stood out to him.

"Walk in My ways."

Josiah refused to stay silent. He gathered the people and read the scroll to them. He removed idols from the land and led the nation back to God. A revival began not because Josiah was powerful, but because he listened, repented, and acted even though he was young.

Josiah's story shows that age does not limit influence. God can use a willing heart at any stage of life. Revival often starts with one person who chooses truth.

P
R
A
Y

God, give me a heart that listens to You and courage to live out what I learn, no matter my age.

Reflection

What truth from Scripture has challenged you to change something in your life recently?

24 Job Holds On

Job's life fell apart faster than anyone could imagine. His wealth vanished, his children died, and his health collapsed. Pain covered him physically and emotionally. His friends tried to explain it, offering advice that only made things worse. They told him he must have done something wrong. They misunderstood his suffering completely.

Job did not pretend he was fine. He cried out honestly. He questioned. He struggled. Yet he still held onto one truth, even when he could not feel hope.

"Though He slay me, yet will I trust."

Job's faith was not full of cheerful words. It was full of raw honesty. He brought every emotion to God. He waited even when waiting hurt. He believed God was still good even when his world said otherwise.

In time, God spoke. He reminded Job of His power, His wisdom, and His care over creation. God did not explain every reason for Job's suffering, but He assured Job that He had never abandoned him. That assurance restored Job's strength long before his circumstances changed.

Later, God healed Job and blessed him again, but the restoration was not the point. The point was that faith can survive storms. Faith holds on when answers are unclear.

Job teaches us that God is close to the brokenhearted. He welcomes our questions and our pain. He carries us even when we barely have strength to stand.

P
R *God, stay close to me in my hardest seasons. Remind me*
A *that You are present even when life feels overwhelming.*
Y

Reflection

How has a difficult season shaped your understanding of God's character?

25 The Lord Is My Shepherd

David wrote Psalm 23 during a time of uncertainty, yet the words reveal deep confidence in God. He began with a simple, comforting truth.

"The Lord is my shepherd."

David remembered his own days as a shepherd. He knew how carefully he watched over his sheep, how he guided them, protected them, and provided for their needs. If he cared for animals that much, how much more would God care for him? With that thought, David described what God does for every person who trusts Him.

God leads us beside still waters, places where our minds and hearts can rest. He restores our souls when anxiety drains us. He guides us on the right path when we feel lost or confused. Even in the darkest valleys, God walks beside us. Fear loses power when we remember His presence.

David's words continue with a beautiful image of God preparing a table for us in the presence of our enemies. God covers us with blessing even when life feels hostile. His goodness does not depend on our situation. It follows us everywhere.

Psalm 23 reminds us that God's care is personal, steady, and gentle. He does not rush us. He does not abandon us. He leads us one step at a time.

P
R *God, give me a heart that listens to You and courage to live out*
A *what I learn, no matter my age.*
Y

Reflection

What truth from Scripture has challenged you to change something in your life recently?

26 Jonah Runs and Returns

Jonah was a prophet, but he wanted nothing to do with God's newest assignment. God told him to go to Nineveh, a city known for violence and cruelty. Jonah refused. He boarded a ship headed far in the opposite direction, hoping distance would silence God's call.

But the sea rose against him. Winds roared. Waves crashed over the deck. Sailors threw cargo into the water, terrified the ship would break apart. Jonah knew the truth. He told them quietly, "Pick me up and throw me into the sea." The moment he hit the water, the storm stopped.

Jonah expected his story to end there, swallowed by the depths. But instead, something massive moved beneath him, and the next moment he was inside the belly of a great fish. Darkness pressed around him. Seaweed wrapped near his face. He remembered a line he once prayed in the temple:

"Salvation belongs to the Lord."

Inside that strange and lonely place, Jonah finally prayed honestly. He admitted his fear. He admitted he had run from God. He asked for mercy. After three days, the fish released him onto dry land.

This time Jonah obeyed. He walked into Nineveh and warned the people to turn from their evil ways. Shockingly, they listened. From the king to the common people, everyone repented. God showed mercy, proving His compassion reaches farther than Jonah ever expected.

Jonah's story teaches us that running from God never brings peace. But turning back to Him always brings another chance.

P
R *God, help me respond to Your voice even when obedience feels*
A *difficult. Give me a willing heart that follows where You lead.*
Y

Reflection

What is one area of your life where you may be running from what God is asking you to do?

27 The Fiery Furnace Faith

Shadrach, Meshach, and Abednego lived in Babylon after being taken from their homeland. King Nebuchadnezzar built a massive golden statue and commanded everyone to bow when the music played. Anyone who refused would be thrown into a blazing furnace.

When the music began, everyone bowed except the three young men. Officials reported them to the king, and Nebuchadnezzar demanded they bow immediately. They stood firm and spoke a line that still inspires courage today.

"Our God is able to save."

They added that even if God chose not to rescue them, they would still refuse to bow. Their loyalty to God was stronger than their fear of the furnace. Enraged, the king ordered the fire heated seven times hotter and had them thrown into the flames.

But the soldiers who brought them to the furnace died from the heat. Inside, the king saw something miraculous. He shouted in shock, asking why four men were walking unharmed in the fire instead of three. One looked like a heavenly being.

The three men walked out without even the smell of smoke on their clothes. The king praised God and declared that no other god could save like this.

Their story reminds us that faith is not proven in comfort. It is revealed in pressure. God does not always remove the fire, but He walks with us inside it.

PRAY

God, give me courage to stand firm in my faith even when I feel pressured to blend in or give in.

Reflection

How does knowing God is with you in the fire change the way you face challenges?

28 Daniel's Steadfast Faith

Years after the fiery furnace, Daniel continued serving faithfully under new kings. His character was excellent, his wisdom respected, and his devotion to God unwavering. This made some officials jealous. They searched for corruption in Daniel's life, but found none. So they created a trap.

The king signed a law saying no one could pray to any god or person except the king for thirty days. Daniel heard the law but responded in the most natural way for him. He went to his room, opened his windows toward Jerusalem, and prayed three times a day, just as he always had.

Daniel's enemies caught him and brought him before the king. The king liked Daniel and tried to find a loophole, but the law could not be changed. Daniel was thrown into a lions' den. That night the king barely slept.

Morning came. The king hurried to the den and called out, **"Daniel, has your God rescued you?"** Daniel replied joyfully. God had sent an angel to shut the lions' mouths. Daniel was brought out unharmed.

Daniel's story teaches us that faith is shaped by habits long before trials come. He did not wait for courage to appear. He practiced faith daily until courage became natural.

We stand strongest when prayer is a lifestyle, not an emergency button.

P
R *God, strengthen my daily habits of faith so I can remain steady and*
A *faithful no matter what pressure I face.*
Y

Reflection

What spiritual habit would help your faith stay strong even during difficult seasons?

29 Esther's Courage

Esther lived in Persia at a time when her people faced growing danger. She was chosen as queen, but she kept her Jewish identity secret. Meanwhile, a powerful official named Haman developed a hatred for the Jews and convinced the king to sign a law that would destroy them.

Esther's cousin Mordecai urged her to speak to the king, but approaching the king without an invitation could mean death. Esther felt fear tighten around her heart. She did not feel ready or powerful. But Mordecai reminded her of a truth that still echoes today.

"Who knows but you were made for this?"

Esther asked the people to fast and pray with her. After days of preparation, she approached the king. Instead of punishing her, he held out his golden scepter and welcomed her. Esther invited the king and Haman to a banquet. At the second banquet, she revealed the truth about Haman's evil plan.

The king became furious and ordered justice. The Jewish people were saved, and Esther's courage changed the future of an entire nation.

Her story reminds us that courage does not mean fear disappears. It means doing the right thing even while our hearts race. God places each of us in certain moments for a reason, even when we do not feel ready.

P
R *God, give me courage when responsibility feels heavy. Help me step*
A *into the moments You created me for with faith instead of fear.*
Y

Reflection

What situation in your life might require courage that you have been avoiding?

30 Nehemiah Rebuilds

Nehemiah lived in Persia, serving the king as a cupbearer. One day he received heartbreaking news. Jerusalem's walls were broken, its gates burned, and its people discouraged. The city that once reflected God's glory lay in ruins. Nehemiah sat down and wept.

He prayed a simple but powerful line.

"Remember Your promise."

Nehemiah asked God for favor, and God answered. The king granted him permission to go to Jerusalem and even supplied the materials needed to rebuild. When Nehemiah arrived, he inspected the ruined walls at night. The task looked overwhelming, but he encouraged the people, telling them God was with them.

They began rebuilding immediately. Enemies tried to stop them with threats, insults, and fear. Some workers built while others held swords. Nehemiah kept reminding them not to give up. His confidence came not from strength, but from faith.

The people persevered, and in just fifty-two days the wall was finished. What had been broken for years became whole again because a leader chose prayer, courage, and determination.

Nehemiah's story teaches us that God often uses ordinary people to accomplish extraordinary restoration. Rebuilding is never easy, whether it is a city, a relationship, or a hurting heart. But God equips those who are willing to begin, even when the task looks impossible.

P
R *God, help me rebuild the broken areas of my life with courage and*
A *faith. Strengthen my hands when the work feels overwhelming.*
Y

Reflection

What "broken wall" in your life or relationships needs rebuilding right now?

31 Hope Is Born

Bethlehem was crowded the night Jesus entered the world. Travelers filled every home, every spare corner, leaving Mary and Joseph with nowhere to stay. They settled in a stable, where the warm breath of animals filled the air. It was there, in the quiet darkness, that Mary gave birth to a child who would change everything.

Angels announced the news to shepherds watching their sheep nearby. Light burst around them, and a voice filled the sky with a message that shook their hearts awake:

"Glory to God in the highest."

The shepherds hurried toward Bethlehem, running through the night until they found the baby lying in a manger.

Jesus did not arrive with trumpets or palaces. He arrived in humility. A tiny infant wrapped in cloth. The King of Kings beginning His life among ordinary people. Everything about His birth whispered hope. Hope for the broken. Hope for the lonely. Hope for the world.

Mary treasured every moment. Joseph stood close, protective and steady. They knew this child carried a greater purpose than they could understand. As morning approached, shepherds spread the news joyfully. Everyone who heard their story felt wonder rise inside them.

The birth of Jesus reminds us that God often steps into our world quietly. He meets us in unexpected places, bringing peace where fear once lived and light where darkness felt heavy. Hope began in a manger, and it still reaches us today.

P R A Y

God, thank You for sending Jesus in a way that shows Your love reaches the humble and the ordinary. Let His hope fill my heart today.

Reflection

Which part of the Christmas story reminds you most that God notices the ordinary and overlooked?

32 Jesus Resists Temptation

After Jesus was baptized, He went into the wilderness. No crowds. No comfort. No food for forty days. The silence was deep, and hunger pressed hard. In that weakness, the tempter approached Him with offers meant to distract Him from His mission.

First, Satan pointed to the stones and urged Jesus to turn them into bread. Jesus refused, remembering the words He had long known: "Man shall not live by bread alone." His identity was grounded in God, not in proving His power.

Then Satan took Him to a high place and showed Him the kingdoms of the world. He promised Jesus authority and glory if He bowed in worship. Jesus answered with truth that cut through the lie: **"You shall worship the Lord."** His loyalty was not for sale.

Finally, Satan took Jesus to the highest point of the temple and challenged Him to jump, twisting God's words to make the temptation sound spiritual. Jesus did not fall for it. He replied firmly, "You shall not test God," choosing trust over spectacle.

After Satan left, angels came and tended to Him. Jesus walked out of the wilderness stronger, prepared to begin His ministry.

His victory shows us that temptation does not mean weakness. It means we are human. Jesus faced every pressure we feel, yet He overcame through truth, identity, and trust. His example teaches us that we can resist temptation not by strength alone, but by holding tightly to God's Word.

P
R *God, help me respond to temptation with truth. Give me clarity to*
A *recognize lies and strength to choose what honors You.*
Y

Reflection

How can knowing your identity in God help you resist things that pull you off track?

33 A New Way to Live

Crowds gathered on the hillside, curious about the teacher everyone was talking about. Jesus sat down, and His words flowed with a quiet authority that felt different from any religious leader they had heard before. He began with a blessing that turned expectations upside down.

"Blessed are the pure in heart."

People listened closely. They were used to rules and rituals. But Jesus spoke about the heart, the hidden place where motives, fears, and hopes live. He taught that anger harms relationships long before outward actions show it. He said forgiveness should reach farther than comfort allows. He said love should extend even to enemies.

Jesus told them to let their good works shine in a way that pointed others toward God, not toward themselves. He taught them to trust God for daily needs, to pray with sincerity, and to let go of anxiety because God cares for every small detail. His message was simple but challenging: live in a way that reflects God's love.

People walked away from the mountain with a new understanding. Faith was not just about behavior. It was about becoming people who lived with mercy, peace, honesty, and humility. Jesus showed them a better path, a life shaped from the inside out.

His words still guide us today. They call us to deeper kindness, gentler responses, and stronger trust. They invite us to see the world differently, and to live in a way that brings light wherever we go.

P
R
A
Y

God, shape my heart to reflect Your love. Help me live out Jesus' teachings in everyday choices and conversations.

Reflection

Which teaching from Jesus challenges you the most in daily life?

34 The Storm Becomes Still

Jesus and His disciples stepped into a boat to cross the lake. The water was calm at first, and night settled gently around them. Jesus, exhausted from teaching and healing, lay down in the boat and fell asleep. The disciples rowed quietly until dark clouds rolled in without warning.

The wind grew fierce. Waves crashed over the boat. Water filled the floorboards. Panic took over as the storm raged. The disciples shook Jesus awake, shouting over the thunder, "Do You not care that we are perishing?"

Jesus stood, steady and calm. He looked at the waves towering over them and spoke a simple command.

"Peace, be still."

The wind stopped instantly. The water smoothed out like glass. The storm vanished as quickly as it came. Silence rested on the lake, and the disciples stared in stunned awe.

Their fear shifted to wonder. "Who is this, that the wind obeys Him?" They realized Jesus was not just a wise teacher. He carried authority over nature itself.

This moment shows us that storms do not scare Jesus. Whether the storm is outside or inside us, He remains calm. He responds not with panic but with peace. Sometimes He quiets the storm. Sometimes He quiets our hearts while the storm continues.

The disciples learned that fear shrinks when faith grows. And faith grows when we remember who is in the boat with us.

P R A Y

God, calm the storms in my heart and remind me that You remain steady even when everything around me feels chaotic.

Reflection

What storm in your life are you asking Jesus to speak peace over right now?

35 The Woman Finds Identity

Jesus passed through Samaria on a long journey and sat beside a well in the heat of the day. A woman came alone to draw water, avoiding the crowds who judged her. She expected silence. Instead, Jesus spoke to her, surprising her with kindness.

"Give Me a drink."

She hesitated. Jews and Samaritans rarely spoke to each other, and she was used to being dismissed. But Jesus continued, offering her something far deeper than water. He told her He could give **"living water,"** something that would fill the empty places in her heart.

The woman asked questions, trying to understand. Jesus revealed knowledge about her life, things she thought no one should know. His words were gentle, not condemning. She realized He saw her fully yet treated her with dignity. It was then her identity shifted. She had always been the woman others whispered about, but now she felt known and valued.

The woman dropped her water jar and ran back to town. She told everyone she met about Jesus. People who once avoided her listened eagerly because her voice carried a newfound confidence.

Her encounter shows us that Jesus sees beyond our mistakes and reputations. He sees who we can become. Identity is not shaped by labels or failures. It is shaped by the One who knows us completely and loves us deeply.

P
R *God, help me find my true identity in Your love rather than in the*
A *opinions or judgments of others.*
Y

Reflection

What label or opinion from others have you carried that Jesus may be inviting you to release?

36 The Good Neighbor

A lawyer approached Jesus one day, trying to test Him with a difficult question. "Who is my neighbor?" he asked, hoping for an argument or a technical answer. Instead, Jesus told a story that cut straight to the heart.

A man was traveling from Jerusalem to Jericho when robbers attacked him. They beat him, stripped him, and left him half dead on the road. A priest came by and saw him but crossed to the other side. A Levite arrived next and did the same. Both were religious leaders, yet neither stopped.

Then a Samaritan traveled down the same road. Samaritans and Jews usually avoided each other, but compassion stirred in his heart. He climbed off his animal, cleaned the man's wounds, and wrapped them gently. He lifted the injured man onto his own donkey and brought him to an inn. Before leaving, he told the innkeeper, "Take care of him," and promised to return.

The Samaritan did not act for recognition. He acted because mercy lived inside him. His kindness revealed the meaning of Jesus' words: **"Love your neighbor as yourself."**

Jesus finished the story by asking the lawyer who acted like a neighbor. The answer was obvious. The one who showed mercy.

The story teaches us that love is measured by action, not background. Kindness crosses boundaries and sees people with God's eyes.

P
R *God, help me notice the needs around me and respond with*
A *compassion, even when it costs time, comfort, or convenience.*
Y

Reflection

What makes it challenging for you to show kindness to people who are different from you?

37 The Returning Son

A young man approached his father one day and asked for his share of the inheritance, even though his father was still alive. He wanted freedom without responsibility. The father divided his property and watched his son walk away toward a distant country.

Life felt exciting at first. Parties. Friends. Fast spending. But soon the money disappeared, and famine swept the land. The son found himself caring for pigs, hungry enough to eat the food they ate. It was then he remembered a line from his father's house that echoed in his heart: "There is bread enough."

With shame weighing him down, he began the long walk home. He rehearsed apologies, unsure if his father would even let him near the house. But while he was still far off, his father saw him. Love moved the father to run toward him. He threw his arms around his son, not waiting for explanations.

The son began to speak, but the father called for celebration. A robe. A ring. Sandals. A feast. The son expected punishment. Instead, he found grace.

His brother struggled to accept this forgiveness, but the father simply said, **"My son was lost and is found."** The father's love was big enough for both sons, whether rebellious or resentful.

The story reminds us that God runs toward us long before we fix ourselves. Coming home begins with honesty and ends with grace.

P
R *God, help me return to You with honesty. Teach me to receive Your*
A *grace instead of hiding in shame.*
Y

Reflection

Which character in this story do you relate to most right now: the younger son, the older brother, or the father?

38 Zacchaeus Changes Direction

Zacchaeus was known in Jericho for the wrong reasons. As a chief tax collector, he had taken money unfairly for years. People avoided him. They whispered about him behind his back. But something about Jesus drew him. When Jesus came through the city, Zacchaeus wanted to see Him, but the crowd was too large and Zacchaeus was too short.

He ran ahead and climbed a sycamore tree. Perched on a branch, he hoped to get a glimpse. When Jesus reached the tree, He stopped, looked up, and called him by name. "Zacchaeus, hurry and come down." Zacchaeus was stunned. He climbed down quickly and welcomed Jesus joyfully.

People grumbled. They could not understand why Jesus would visit someone like him. But Jesus looked at Zacchaeus with compassion, seeing possibility instead of reputation. Something shifted inside Zacchaeus. He stood and made a promise that surprised everyone: **"I give half my goods to the poor."** He added that anyone he had wronged would be repaid four times over.

His words showed a true change of heart. Jesus declared, "Salvation has come to this house," because transformation had taken root.

Zacchaeus' story reminds us that no one is too far from grace. A single moment of being seen by Jesus can redirect a life completely.

P
R *God, open my heart to real change. Help me turn from harmful*
A *choices and walk in the new direction You show me.*
Y

Reflection

What change in your life would show others that your heart is growing?

39 Jesus Serves First

On the night before His crucifixion, Jesus and His disciples gathered for a final meal. The room was familiar, yet there was tension in the air. The disciples argued quietly about who among them was the greatest. No one wanted to take the lowest position in the room.

While they talked, Jesus stood up. He took off His outer garment, wrapped a towel around His waist, and poured water into a basin. The disciples fell silent as He knelt beside them. One by one, He washed their feet. The King of Kings took the posture of a servant.

Peter protested, feeling unworthy. But Jesus told him, "If I do not wash you, you have no share with Me." Peter understood that this moment was deeper than clean feet. It was about humility and love.

When Jesus finished, He looked at His disciples and said, **"I have given you an example."**

His message was clear. Leadership in God's kingdom is not about being first. It is about serving others with compassion and humility.

Jesus knew His time was short, yet He chose to serve rather than be served. His love reached into the messy places of life and demonstrated what greatness truly looks like.

The foot-washing reminds us that love is practical. Love bends down. Love acts quietly. Love goes first.

P
R *God, help me choose humility and kindness in my relationships.*
A *Teach me to serve others the way Jesus served His disciples.*
Y

Reflection

Who in your life needs a practical expression of love from you this week?

40 Gethsemane Pressure

After the final meal, Jesus went with His disciples to the Garden of Gethsemane. Night wrapped around them, and the weight of what was coming pressed heavily on His heart. Jesus asked His closest friends to stay awake and pray with Him, but they were exhausted and kept falling asleep.

Jesus moved a little farther into the garden. There, under the olive trees, He prayed with honesty and anguish. His words revealed the depth of His struggle:

"Not My will, but Yours be done."

He felt sorrow that nearly overwhelmed Him, yet He surrendered fully to the Father's plan.

As He prayed, sweat fell like drops of blood to the ground. An angel appeared and strengthened Him, but the battle inside His heart was real. This was not a moment of calm confidence. It was a moment of wrestling, choosing obedience in the midst of fear.

Soldiers soon arrived with torches. Judas led them, and the disciples panicked. But Jesus stepped forward peacefully. He knew the path ahead was painful, yet He chose love over escape.

Gethsemane teaches us that real courage is not the absence of fear. It is choosing God's will even when our emotions pull us in another direction. Jesus understands pressure, loneliness, and internal battles. He knows what it feels like to face something overwhelming.

His strength in the garden gives us hope for our own hardest moments.

P
R A Y

God, meet me in the moments when I feel overwhelmed. Give me the strength to say "Your will be done" even when it is difficult.

Reflection

How does Jesus' struggle in Gethsemane help you understand that faith can include deep emotion and wrestling?

41 Love on the Cross

The sky darkened as Jesus hung on the cross. Crowds mocked Him. Soldiers divided His clothes. Religious leaders watched with cold satisfaction. Yet Jesus looked at the people hurting Him and felt compassion instead of anger. With breath growing harder, He spoke words that revealed His heart:

"Father, forgive them."

Pain shot through His body, but He stayed on the cross because love held Him there. He carried every sin, every failure, every fear, every wound. The weight of the world pressed on Him, yet He chose to stay so we could be free.

Two criminals hung beside Him. One insulted Him, but the other saw the truth. With courage, the criminal whispered a plea. Jesus answered him gently, offering hope even in His final hours: "Today you will be with Me."

As Jesus died, the earth shook. The temple curtain tore from top to bottom, symbolizing that nothing now stood between God and humanity. Love broke every barrier.

A Roman soldier watching everything said what many were thinking: "Truly this was the Son of God." Even the ones who helped crucify Him felt the weight of that moment.

The cross shows us a love deeper than pain, stronger than hatred, and powerful enough to rewrite any story. Jesus gave His life not because He was forced, but because He wanted us close again.

P
R *God, help me understand the depth of Jesus' love on the cross.*
A *Let His sacrifice soften my heart and shape the way I live.*
Y

Reflection

What part of the crucifixion story makes you most aware of how deeply God loves you?

42 The Empty Tomb

Early in the morning, just after the Sabbath, women carried spices to Jesus' tomb. The sky was still pale, and the world felt heavy with grief. They expected silence and a sealed stone. Instead, they found the stone rolled away.

The tomb was empty.

As they stood confused, two angels appeared and asked a question that stirred hope inside their breaking hearts: "Why do you seek the living among the dead?" The women trembled. Something impossible had happened. Jesus was alive.

They ran to tell the disciples, but the men struggled to believe them. Peter and John sprinted to the tomb. John arrived first and saw the linen cloths lying there. Peter stepped inside and saw evidence of a miracle he could barely understand.

Later that day, Jesus appeared to Mary. She recognized Him when He spoke her name. "Mary." One word changed everything. She fell at His feet, tears of joy replacing tears of sorrow.

Jesus also appeared to the disciples in a locked room. Fear turned to amazement as He said, **"Peace be with you."** He showed them His hands and side. Death had been defeated. Hope was alive again.

The empty tomb teaches us that God's power reaches beyond our deepest losses. What feels final to us is not final to Him. Resurrection means new beginnings, restored hope, and a future no darkness can steal.

PRAY

God, thank You for the victory of the resurrection. Help me live with the confidence that nothing is impossible for You.

Reflection

How would your daily life look different if you lived with resurrection-sized confidence?

43 Go and Make Disciples

After His resurrection, Jesus met His disciples on a mountain in Galilee. Some worshiped, some hesitated, and all of them tried to understand what their future would look like without Him physically beside them. Jesus stepped closer and spoke with steady authority.

"All authority in heaven and earth is Mine."

The disciples, once fearful and unsure, listened as He gave them a mission that stretched beyond anything they had imagined. Jesus told them to go into every nation, share His message, baptize people, and teach them everything He had commanded. This mission was not for the talented or the confident. It was for ordinary people transformed by extraordinary grace.

Jesus promised them something powerful before He left. "I am with you always." No distance, culture, or challenge would separate them from His presence. The disciples would not go alone. His Spirit would guide them, strengthen them, and give them courage.

This moment on the mountain launched the greatest movement in history. It spread from fishermen and tax collectors to villages, cities, and entire nations. The message grew because people obeyed with willing hearts.

Jesus' call still stands today. We are invited to live boldly, love deeply, and share hope wherever we go. Our mission is not to be perfect, but to be present.

P
R *God, give me courage to live out the mission Jesus gave.*
A *Help me share Your love with confidence and compassion.*
Y

Reflection

Which part of Jesus' mission feels most challenging for you, and why?

44 Power at Pentecost

Fifty days after Jesus' resurrection, the disciples gathered in an upstairs room in Jerusalem. They prayed, waited, and wondered what Jesus meant when He promised they would receive power. The city below them buzzed with festival crowds, but the room above stayed still.

Suddenly, a sound like rushing wind filled the house. It wasn't ordinary wind. It moved with purpose. Flames appeared and rested above each disciple. In that moment, their fear melted away, and they were filled with the Holy Spirit.

The disciples began speaking in languages they had never learned. People from many nations heard them declaring "the mighty works of God" in their own tongues. Confusion turned to amazement. Thousands gathered to figure out what was happening.

Peter, who once denied Jesus, stood with boldness. His voice carried power as he told the crowd that God had raised Jesus from the dead. His words pierced hearts. By the end of the day, three thousand people decided to follow Jesus.

The church was born.

People shared meals, prayers, and resources. Needs were met. Joy overflowed. The Spirit united them and gave them courage to keep spreading the message.

Pentecost teaches us that God empowers ordinary people to do extraordinary things. Fear becomes courage. Confusion becomes clarity. Hesitation becomes boldness. The Holy Spirit still fills hearts today, guiding us, comforting us, and giving us the strength to live out our faith.

P
R *God, fill me with Your Spirit so I can live with boldness, wisdom,*
A *and love. Help me use Your power for good in the world.*
Y

Reflection

What part of the early church inspires you as you think about your own faith community?

45 Peter Is Restored

Peter had always been bold, the first to speak and the first to step forward. But on the night Jesus was arrested, fear overtook him. Three times he denied knowing Jesus. When the rooster crowed, Peter remembered Jesus' words and wept bitterly.

After the resurrection, Peter carried both hope and shame. He knew Jesus was alive, yet his failure weighed heavily. One morning, while fishing on the Sea of Galilee, Peter saw someone standing on the shore. When the man called out, "Cast your net on the right side," Peter recognized the voice. He jumped into the water and swam to Jesus.

A fire crackled on the shore. Fish cooked. Bread warmed in the early light. After they ate, Jesus looked at Peter and asked gently, "Do you love Me?" Peter answered yes. Jesus asked again. Then a third time. The repeated question touched the place where Peter had failed, not to shame him but to heal him.

Jesus told him, **"Feed My sheep."**

With those words, He restored Peter's calling. The man who once denied Jesus was chosen to help lead the early church.

Peter's story reminds us that failure is not final. Jesus meets us in our broken moments, asks honest questions, and invites us back into purpose. Restoration is His specialty.

P R A Y

God, thank You for meeting me in my failures. Restore the parts of my life that feel damaged, and help me walk forward with confidence.

Reflection

What is one area of your life where you need Jesus' restoration right now?

46 Paul's Transformation

Saul was known for his determination and intensity. He sincerely believed he was honoring God by hunting down followers of Jesus. He dragged believers from their homes, broke apart families, and filled entire communities with fear. His heart was convinced he was right, even as he walked in darkness.

One day he traveled to Damascus with authority to arrest more believers. But as he approached the city, a brilliant light flashed around him. Saul fell to the ground, blinded by power he had never felt before. A voice spoke his name with undeniable clarity:

"Why do you persecute Me?"

Saul trembled. He realized he had been fighting against the very One he claimed to serve. Blinded, he was led into the city where he waited in silence for three days. No sight. No strength. Just reflection.

God sent a believer named Ananias to pray for him. Ananias was afraid, but he went anyway. When he placed his hands on Saul, something like scales fell from Saul's eyes. Sight returned. So did purpose. Saul was baptized and given a new direction.

From that moment on, Saul became Paul, one of the most influential voices in the early church. The man who once tried to destroy the message now carried it across nations. His heart softened. His passion was redeemed.

Paul's story shows that no one is beyond God's reach. One encounter can redirect an entire life. Grace can transform even the hardest heart.

P
R *God, change the parts of my heart that resist You.*
A *Lead me into the purpose You designed for my life.*
Y

Reflection

When have you experienced a moment that completely shifted your perspective?

47 Joy in Chains

Paul spent much of his ministry traveling, teaching, and encouraging new believers. But there came a time when he found himself locked inside a prison cell. Cold stone walls surrounded him. Chains weighed on his wrists. Many would have given up hope, but Paul saw the situation differently.

Instead of despair, he chose joy.

He wrote letters to churches, reminding them that God was still working. He urged them to rejoice, even in hardship. One phrase he wrote from that dark cell continues to lift hearts today:

"Rejoice in the Lord always."

Paul did not ignore suffering. He felt every restriction and every moment of discomfort. But he believed that joy came not from circumstances, but from God's presence. Guards watched him closely. Some probably expected complaints or anger. Instead, Paul prayed, sang, and encouraged everyone who visited him.

His attitude made an impact. People who never would have heard about Jesus learned through Paul's example that faith shines brightest in difficult places. Even chains could not silence hope.

Paul's story reminds us that joy is not fragile. It does not depend on comfort or success. It grows when we trust that God is still near, still working, and still good.

P
R
A
Y

God, teach me to find joy in every season, not because life is perfect, but because You are with me.

Reflection

Where do you find it hardest to choose joy, and why?

48 The Spirit's Fruit

The early believers were learning how to live differently now that the Holy Spirit guided them. Life in the Spirit did not look like following a list of rules. It looked like allowing God to shape their character from the inside out. Paul described it with simple, beautiful clarity using a phrase that many still know by heart:

"The fruit of the Spirit."

This fruit was not something people could manufacture on their own. It grew naturally in hearts surrendered to God. Love that did not depend on approval. Joy that did not collapse in hardship. Peace that held steady through chaos. Patience that refused to rush. Kindness that noticed others. Goodness that acted with integrity. Faithfulness that stayed steady. Gentleness that softened harshness. Self-control that chose wisdom over impulse.

Paul wanted believers to see that spiritual maturity is not measured by talent or achievement. It is measured by character. The more a person walks with God, the more these qualities appear.

This fruit does not grow overnight. It forms slowly, the way fruit ripens on a tree. Even small progress matters. A kinder response. A patient moment. A choice to forgive. All of it reveals God's work inside us.

The Spirit's fruit shows the world what God's love looks like in real life.

P
R *God, give me a heart that listens to You and courage to live out*
A *what I learn, no matter my age.*
Y

Reflection

Which fruit of the Spirit do you most want to grow in right now, and why?

49 The Armor of God

Paul knew believers faced pressures, temptations, and spiritual battles that could not be fought with physical weapons. Life brought doubts, fears, lies, and discouragement. To help believers stand firm, Paul used a powerful image: armor.

He described truth like a belt that holds everything in place. He pictured righteousness as a breastplate guarding the heart. He spoke of peace as shoes that help us stand steady. He described faith as a shield that can extinguish attacks. He called salvation a helmet protecting the mind. And he pictured God's Word as a sword that brings clarity and strength.

One line captures his encouragement with simple power:

"Be strong in the Lord."

Paul wanted people to understand that strength does not come from willpower alone. It comes from leaning on God. The armor was not meant to make believers intimidating, but protected. It showed that God equips His people for every challenge they face.

This armor is not something we put on once. It is a daily way of living. Choosing truth over lies. Choosing peace over panic. Choosing faith over fear. Choosing God's voice over the loud noise of the world.

The armor of God reminds us that we are not defenseless. With God's protection, we can stand firm, even in difficult seasons.

P
R *God, help me put on Your armor each day. Strengthen me to face*
A *challenges with faith, peace, and truth.*
Y

Reflection

How does knowing God equips you change the way you handle spiritual or emotional battles?

50 The New Creation

John received a vision while exiled on the island of Patmos. He was alone, surrounded by rocky cliffs and crashing waves, yet God opened his eyes to see the future. What he saw was breathtaking. A restored world, perfect and whole. A place where brokenness no longer existed and sadness had no home.

John saw a new heaven and a new earth. He described a holy city, bright as crystal. The voice he heard declared a promise filled with hope:

"Behold, I make all things new."

In this new creation, God lived among His people forever. There was no more death, mourning, crying, or pain. Every tear was wiped away by God Himself. Light replaced darkness. Peace replaced fear. Joy replaced sorrow.

The beauty of the new world reminded John that God's story does not end in suffering. It ends in restoration. Every loss we experience on earth will be answered with fullness. Every wrong will be made right. Every wound will be healed.

This vision invites us to hope even in difficult seasons. The future God is preparing is filled with brightness beyond our imagination. Faithfulness today connects us to that future joy.

The new creation reminds us that God always finishes what He begins. His love carries us not only through this life, but into the life to come.

P
R *God, thank You for the hope of a restored world. Help me live with*
A *my eyes on eternity and with faith that You make all things new.*
Y

Reflection

How might living with eternity in mind change the way you handle everyday challenges?

An Introduction to All the Books

Genesis	God creates the world and begins His rescue plan.
Exodus	God frees Israel and teaches them how to follow Him.
Leviticus	Instructions for worship and living close to God.
Numbers	Israel's journey through the wilderness.
Deuteronomy	Moses' reminders before entering the Promised Land.
Joshua	Israel enters the land and God gives victory.
Judges	A cycle of failure, rescue, and God's patience.
Ruth	A story of loyalty, kindness, and God's provision.
1 Samuel	Samuel, Saul, and the rise of David.
2 Samuel	David's reign with highs, lows, and God's mercy.
1 Kings	Solomon's wisdom and Israel's divided kingdom.
2 Kings	The fall of Israel and Judah.
1 Chronicles	David's life retold with focus on worship.
2 Chronicles	Kings of Judah and God's faithfulness.
Ezra	Returning from exile and rebuilding the temple.
Nehemiah	Rebuilding Jerusalem's walls.
Esther	God protects His people through Esther's courage.
Job	Why suffering happens and how God meets us in it.
Psalms	Songs and prayers for every emotion.
Proverbs	Practical wisdom for everyday life.
Ecclesiastes	Searching for meaning beyond temporary things.
Song of Solomon	A poetic celebration of love.
Isaiah	Warnings, hope, and prophecies of the Messiah.
Jeremiah	A call to return to God.
Lamentations	Honest grief over Jerusalem's destruction.
Ezekiel	Visions reminding Israel that God is still in control.
Daniel	Faithfulness in a foreign land.
Hosea	God's faithful love toward unfaithful people.
Joel	A warning and a hope-filled promise.
Amos	God stands for justice and righteousness.
Obadiah	Judgment for Edom's pride.
Jonah	God's mercy reaches even enemies.
Micah	Justice, humility, and hope in God.
Nahum	God brings justice against cruelty.
Habakkuk	Trusting God through confusion.

Zephaniah	Judgment and restoration.
Haggai	A call to rebuild God's house.
Zechariah	Visions of encouragement for God's people.
Malachi	A final call to return to God before Jesus comes.
Matthew	Jesus as the promised Messiah.
Mark	Jesus' power shown through action.
Luke	Jesus' compassion and humanity highlighted.
John	Jesus as the Son of God who brings life.
Acts	The early church empowered by the Spirit.
Romans	The foundation of salvation and grace.
1 Corinthians	Guidance for a struggling church.
2 Corinthians	Encouragement and strength in weakness.
Galatians	Freedom through Christ alone.
Ephesians	Identity, unity, and spiritual strength.
Philippians	Joy in every season.
Colossians	Jesus is above everything.
1 Thessalonians	Encouragement and hope.
2 Thessalonians	Staying faithful under pressure.
1 Timothy	Leadership and wisdom for young pastors.
2 Timothy	Finishing strong in faith.
Titus	Building strong, healthy churches.
Philemon	Forgiveness and restored relationships.
Hebrews	Jesus is the perfect sacrifice and priest.
James	Faith that shows through action.
1 Peter	Hope in suffering.
2 Peter	Standing strong against false teachings.
1 John	Living in truth and love.
2 John	Staying loyal to Christ.
3 John	Supporting faithful believers.
Jude	Defending the truth.
Revelation	God wins. New creation begins

Key Bible Concepts

Grace is God giving us what we could never earn.
Faith means trusting God even when we cannot see the outcome.
Repentance is turning away from sin and turning toward God with honesty.
Salvation is a gift of God rescuing us from sin through Jesus.
Forgiveness means releasing bitterness and giving to others the same grace God gives us.
Prayer is a conversation with God.
When we follow Jesus, our identity is rooted in Him, not in labels, mistakes, or opinions.
The Holy Spirit guides, comforts, strengthens, and transforms us from the inside out.
Love is the defining mark of a follower of Jesus. It is action, not emotion.
Hope is confidence that God keeps His promises, even when life feels uncertain.

How to Read the Bible

A helpful way to read is the familiar SOAP method:

S - Scripture:
Write down a verse or section that catches your attention.
O - Observation:
What is happening? What stands out? What does this show about God or people?
A - Application:
How can this verse shape your choices, attitude, or thinking today?
P - Prayer:
Talk to God honestly about what you learned and what you need.

Use a translation that is clear and teen-friendly. If something is confusing, don't stop. The more you show up, the more familiar His voice becomes. Small daily readings create spiritual growth over time.